What others are saying about *The Same Page*

"*The Same Page* taps into the innermost thoughts and desires of every girl, no matter her age. *The Same Page* is a beautiful narrative discussion about real issues facing mothers and daughters in our world today."

—Lauren Nelson
Miss America 2007

"Though Shauna Pilgreen and Courtney Bullard wrote *The Same Page* as a fairy tale for women, it's far more! With the enchantment and wonder of great storytelling, the authors weave a charming and engaging tale that speaks directly to the reality in which women live and awakens the possibility of a greater reality they long for. Every woman wants to know she is seen by the King, and this narrative reminds a woman's heart that she is seen and known. It also provides hope that the King can bring restoration in the relationships between mothers and daughters and between women and their God.

"*The Same Page* taps into that delightful place in a woman's heart she never tires of revisiting—that place of girlish wonder. It grants far more than a good read; it facilitates an enchanting experience—especially when shared between a mother and her daughter.

"The journal pages in *The Same Page* take it past being a mere tale and prompt the reader to make it her story. Journaling allows her to inscribe her story in the pages of this story so she can experience God's story.

"I have full confidence in Shauna and Courtney as trustworthy and capable raconteurs, who not only tell a great story for mothers and daughters but tell God's great story for all women."

—Jennifer Rothschild

Author of five books, including *Lessons I Learned in the Dark, Self Talk, Soul Talk,* and three Bible studies; founder of Fresh Grounded Faith conferences.

"In our culture, mother-in-law/daughter-in-law is usually the most strained relationship. Mother/daughter runs a close second. This book from Courtney and Shauna can help temper this difficult interaction. Read this book with your daughter when she's in preschool. Read it together again when she's in grade school. Read it together again when she becomes a teenager. Read it together again when she's an adult. Encourage your daughter to read it often with her daughter. This book helps."

—Dr. John Marshall

Senior Pastor, Springfield, Missouri
Second Baptist Church

"God has decreed that spiritual truths are to 'be upon the hearts of' mothers. Then, mothers are to 'impress them' on their daughters—when they 'walk along the road, when (they) lie down and… get up.' But mothers and daughters also are to share truth when they 'sit at home.' Courtney Bullard and Shauna Pilgreen have given mothers and daughters a delightful way to do just that. *The Same Page* wraps truth in an engaging world of castles, balls, and dreams. I am certain that as both generations move through this reading and sharing experience, they will come to adore their true King in ways they never have before."

—Richard Ross, PhD

Professor of Student Ministry, Southwestern Seminary, Co-founder, True Love Waits

"Someone very wise once said that there are two great days in a person's life: the day you were born and the day you realize why. As the father of two daughters, I pray most that our girls will live from purpose and passion and not from some confused, twisted perspective that seems to ooze from culture. Courtney and Shauna have their finger on this pulse and dive fearlessly into the deep end with this incredible resource for teenage girls and mothers. Weaving masterful story with powerful principle, this book drills to the heart of what I consider the most important issue for every girl on planet earth."

—Stuart Hall

Author of *Seven Checkpoints: 7 Principles Every Teenager Needs to Know, Max Q: Developing Students of Influence,* and *Wired: For a Life of Worship*

The Same Page

The Same Page

....

Living Your Happily Ever After

Courtney Bullard & Shauna Pilgreen

TATE PUBLISHING
AND ENTERPRISES, LLC

The Same Page
Copyright © 2012 by Courtney Bullard & Shauna Pilgreen. All rights reserved.

No part of this publication may be reproduced, stored in a retrieval system or transmitted in any way by any means, electronic, mechanical, photocopy, recording or otherwise without the prior permission of the author except as provided by USA copyright law.

This novel is a work of fiction. Names, descriptions, entities and incidents included in the story are products of the author's imagination. Any resemblance to actual persons, events and entities is entirely coincidental.

Scripture quotations are from The Holy Bible, English Standard Version® (ESV®), copyright © 2001 by Crossway, a publishing ministry of Good News Publishers. Used by permission. All rights reserved.

The opinions expressed by the author are not necessarily those of Tate Publishing, LLC.

Published by Tate Publishing & Enterprises, LLC
127 E. Trade Center Terrace | Mustang, Oklahoma 73064 USA
1.888.361.9473 | www.tatepublishing.com

Tate Publishing is committed to excellence in the publishing industry. The company reflects the philosophy established by the founders, based on Psalm 68:11,
"The Lord gave the word and great was the company of those who published it."

Book design copyright © 2012 by Tate Publishing, LLC. All rights reserved.
Cover and interior design by Chris Webb
Illustrations by Rebecca Riffey

Published in the United States of America

ISBN: 978-1-62024-561-3
1. Fiction / Christian / General
2. Juvenile Fiction / Historical / Medieva
12.01.17

Dedication

To the women who have poured into our lives
so that we can pour into the lives of others.

To those who helped make my dreams come true . . .

First, to my husband, Steve: you are my backbone, my strength, my better half. Thank you for always listening and at least acting like you care about every single detail.

To my fabulous "go go" daughter, Francesca: you not only make my heart smile but make me laugh out loud every day. What an honor to be your mommy.

To Ron and Linda Smith: I love you, Mom and Dad! You have always been my biggest fans. Thank you for loving me unconditionally and for always supporting and believing in me.

To Shauna Pilgreen: sister, we did it! I couldn't image doing this project with anyone else. Truly the same Spirit in both of us! Amazing how Jesus can bring people together as if we have known each other our entire lives.

To the entire Tate staff: you have been fabulous to work with in making this book a success!

To my prayer warriors: you played a huge role in this entire process. We couldn't have made it through without you and your prayers!

To the I.D. Ministries ladies: it is an honor to do ministry together and show the love of Christ to teenage girls! You are truly Fearless Warriors!

To the Brady Ladies: thank you for being my sisters, for always listening, for your prayers, for your support, and your unconditional love. We are overcomers!

To my entire family: thank you for setting the bar high on what a Christ-minded family should look and act like.

And most importantly: thank you, Jesus, for giving us the vision, motivation, direction, and encouragement we needed to make this dream become a reality. You are the One who puts the words on the pages and who truly sees us!

—Courtney Belle Bullard

Foreword from the King

My child, I love you. I adore you and truly know you better than anyone, including yourself. I know everything about you, and it doesn't change the way I see you or My love for you. Even though you sometimes run from Me, search out other things in My place, and even turn your back on Me, I am still here. I will never leave you. I will never forget you. I want to meet you right where you are. You have My full attention.

I am the King of all kings. I am the God who sees: El-Roi. I do see you. I can be trusted. I have come to offer you hope, forgiveness, and a love like no other. You are magnificent. You are My creation and I never stop thinking about you.

How do you see Me? What do you call Me? Come and sit with Me. I have so many things to reveal to you.

—King El-Roi

So she called the name of the Lord who spoke to her, "You are a God of seeing," for she said, "Truly here I have seen him who looks after me."

—Genesis 16:13

The Pages of Ysabel

In what seems to be forever and a day, I find myself sitting on my mother's old chest, gazing out my window into the fields, wondering if this is all I can expect of my life. There has to be more. Although I feel like I will never be old enough to make my own decisions and live out my dreams, I won't stop trying. As a fifteen-year-old girl living in the village, facing all that medieval life has to offer, sometimes the pressure of watching castle living seems overwhelming. One can look up and see castles surrounding the valley of villages that are separated by a large pasture. The castles always seem to look down upon the village and continually remind us of what we don't have.

I hear the loud voice that so often plays in my head: *Who am I?* I watch the other girls walking the cobblestone roads and wonder where I fit in. There are the cheerleaders of the jousting team, with their lemon juice–

bleached hair, and the girls who always have the latest fashions, usually found in magazines such as *Not Your Average Medieval Girl*. Then there are the popular girls who always have a boyfriend. And of course, the girls who dress a little different from everyone else. I am most drawn to this crowd with my straight black hair and a wardrobe that mostly consists of dark colors. My lips are a blood-red color that I have stained from many painful lemon-rubbing sessions. Am I pursuing this look only to fit into a certain crowd? Being fifteen is hard enough, and the pressures of turning sixteen are worse.

When a girl turns sixteen there is a huge party to celebrate her legal right to enter into the period of making her own decisions. And for a village girl like me, the pressure of being accepted and proving myself seems all the more difficult. Even though my family falls short of the status that gets you a messenger-delivered invitation to the ball, I am excited about entering into this age of independence. I can finally ride my horse unaccompanied and begin my dream of making dresses that

· The Same Page ·

show girls' different styles and reveal their ankles. I awake into reality by my mother's voice. "Ysabel, take your head out of the clouds and come downstairs!" I find myself rolling my eyes once again at my mother.

Why does she always have to treat me like a child? Why can't she be like my best friend's mother? She is so fun and always seems to understand me, unlike my own mother.

As I quickly glance at my reflection in the mirror, I can't help but begin to pick apart the things I see. I hate so many things about my image. Why is my body shaped like this? Why this nose? And why do my lips seem out of proportion? I quickly shake my head, trying to remove the image that stares back at me every day, and run downstairs.

I find my mother, Adela, sweeping the floor. Her hair is a mess, sweat is running down her neck, and her dress is dirty and torn at the bottom. I wonder why she can't fix her hair and smell nice like the castle mothers. Even the castles themselves have a smell of honeysuckle and nectar in the air. My home always smells sweaty and musty.

"Ysabel!" my mother yells again.

"I'm right here! You don't have to yell," I quickly reply.

"Don't just stand there. There is so much work to be done," my mother says to me. Why does she seem so frustrated?

I can almost repeat word for word what she will say even before it comes out of her mouth. How many times have I heard this before? She always acts like I do nothing around here. Does my mother think I'm her slave?

"Mother, I've already cleaned my room. Why do I have to clean downstairs too? This is not my house."

"Ysabel, as long as you live under this roof that your father and I put over your head, then you will do as I say and help with the chores. You need to be grateful for what you have."

Grateful? Grateful for living in the village and not a castle? There is nothing to be grateful about!

"The castle girls are taught by tutors and don't have to get their books from the library.

The Same Page

They own them," I argue. "They are served meals on silver platters and are not out back picking their food. Their fathers buy them whatever they want and are not away in some remote village making cents for a day's work."

She then hands me a brush, and I begin scrubbing potatoes.

"Do you have no appreciation for what you've been given, Ysabel?"

"Of course I do, but, Mother—"

She interrupts me. "Your father is doing all he can to provide a better life for us. He wishes he could be at home, and I know you know that deep in your heart. I'm doing all I can so we can go and buy that gown for the ball."

I know it's a sensitive subject, but I bring it up again.

"Mother, why can't I make my own? I've got it all sketched out. You'd just have to purchase the fabric and—"

"You need to realize something early on, my dear. Your sketches will not put food on the table. You need to get your head out of the clouds and into a trade that will get you further in life." Once again, my mother crushes my dreams.

"What? Like you have a trade that's taking you further in life?"

"Now, listen here. You think you're lacking, Ysabel. I've been pulling potatoes since I was six years old. I went to work for a baker at the age of nine. I want you to live the life I only dreamed of." My mother sounds like a noisy gong.

I want my freedom. When I have children, I am not going to make them work so hard.

"Well, maybe that's not what I have in mind!" I have to get out of this house. I quickly make my way to the front door and slam it as hard as I can. The door takes me by surprise at how loud it is. The entire house seems to shake. Should I go back inside and apologize? No. She wouldn't understand, and I need to cool off.

As I walk the fields, I begin thinking about my father and missing him terribly. He has been gone now for a couple of weeks. My father is a hardworking man but receives very little money. He often travels

The Same Page

to other villages in hopes of receiving more coins for his labor. Although more coins occasionally come in, he is gone from home for months at a time. I absolutely love my father and miss him when he is gone. He seems to understand me, unlike my mother. He is a strong man whose hands are always rough and calloused from the fields. My mother's hands have also become rough and calloused since she takes care of the land in his absence. Has my mother's heart become calloused and hardened as well? Does she know how much I am hurting inside?

One thing that is very apparent is the strong love my mother and father have for each other. My mother is different when my father is around. I often find them dancing together in the kitchen as my father sings in my mother's ear. I love watching them dance and laugh together. I hope one day to have a love like theirs to call my own.

The next morning I proceed out into the fields to pick potatoes, but my mind wanders to greener pastures. I dream of the future; anything has to be better than the present. As I think about my wedding day, my dream of owning my own boutique, and being treated like an adult, my mind comes back to the nearing event, the sweet-sixteen ball. Now this isn't like any other ball, for it is the event of all events. A girl's social status and reputation are determined by the sweet-sixteen ball she attends. Each castle in the land has a sweet-sixteen ball on the same night. Once per year the village and castle girls come together to

The Same Page

celebrate their coming of age, but only if an invitation is received.

The Proper Castle's ball is one of etiquette, high class, drinking fine tea with pinkies lifted in the air and noses raised high. Flutes and stringed instruments play as girls stroll back and forth, saying, "You look lovely today," and "Thank you, so do you."

The Chic Castle has all the latest styles and trends that cost way more than the material itself. The girls wear only designer names and enjoy flashing their Poach handbags, Juiceless shoes, and DeDe dresses. Nothing goes unnoticed, and everyone recognizes what name the others have on.

The Fickle Castle is a very popular one. Every young lady has to have a boy by her side to enter into this sweet-sixteen ball. Girls' laughter resounds as they try to impress the opposite sex. Single ladies are not allowed.

The Gothic Castle welcomes those who march to the beat of a different drum. They know how to party, and this is where I hope to attend. They wear dark colors, and their hair covers the majority of their faces. Drinking is the focus of the party, with wild dancing and smoking of the medieval herb plant.

There are many more castles, but all have one thing in common; they represent something that others are striving to achieve. Some will be tempted to go to every castle, just to try them out and see if it is what they are looking for. Sometimes villagers will work their entire lives trying to attain what castle living has to offer. I know what I want. With that thought, I finish up my chores and hurry inside to get ready for the night. It is obvious that my mother has plans for me to attend the Proper Castle ball. My mother has been so preoccupied with ensuring I have the perfect dress, the perfect hair, and the perfect appearance. She is consumed with the thought of me attending the sweet-sixteen ball at the Proper Castle. My mother has even made comments in passing that she is sure I will meet the perfect man, become all that she knows I can be that is perfect, and fall in love with all the perfect things. If I hear the word perfect one more time I will scream.

· *The Same Page* ·

What my mother doesn't know is that the Gothic Castle is in my forecast, with the handsome Blade controlling my thoughts. I will do whatever it takes to get what I want, for I am independent and can make my own decisions.

My mother has picked out a white gown for me to wear to the Proper Castle. Although it is not my style, I can't help but recognize its beauty. The gown is white, covers my body all the way up to my neck, and reaches down to my heels. The sleeves are tight at the wrists and full at the top. With the right embellishments, I could give this dress a whole new look. It has so much potential, but I lack the resources and permission. I take one final look in the mirror, shrug my shoulders and think, *This will do.*

....

I know my mother is wondering what's taking so long, so I make my way downstairs.

"Well, it's the night of all nights. How do I look?" I spin around and can't help but feel for a moment like a princess twirling in her royal gown. I notice my mother has a smile on her face, but as she looks me over, her smile quickly turns to a frown.

"This will not work. Go bring me your hairbrush, and let's get your hair out of your face."

I hate it when she does this. My mother always seems to find something about me to fix. Why can't she just compliment instead of criticize?

I allow her to begin fixing me into her image of perfection. She pulls my hair smoothly back into a tight bun and places lacings of flowers perfectly in my hair. My mother ensures that my fingernails are trimmed and very clean, and I notice she

The Same Page

seems so happy. Is she crying? Why would she be crying?

"I remember a time when I wore a dress like this and my hair was very similar. I see a little of me in you, Ysabel. Your father would be so proud of you tonight. You know that, don't you?"

"Yes, Mother. Now why the bun? This is so old looking."

"Young lady, a certain style is required at this ball, and we don't want to mess it up. Not every girl in the village will go to a ball tonight. Just think. We could be celebrating your sweet sixteen with cookies and tea just up the road at Clarice's house."

"Mother," I groan.

"Tonight, you could befriend a sweet girl who lives the castle life, meet a respectable young man, and impress families of prominence that might offer you an apprenticeship in town. Endless possibilities, my child."

My mother has now moved on from my hair to smoothing out any wrinkle that may be found on my gown. I can only tolerate this a little longer.

"Mother, come on."

"You're right, Ysabel. You are beautiful and look like an angel. This is the big night when everything is going to be made perfect. Who knows what will become of you after the ball tonight?"

My mother finally stops trying to perfect me, and I make my way to the door. I hold the door open as she practically skips through it.

"We've got to get these cakes to the castle!" my mother says with excitement in her voice.

I have not told anyone the truth about how I am getting to go to the sweet-sixteen ball. All the castle girls are invited, but every once in a while, village girls magically appear. I am one of these village girls tonight. My mother has an amazing talent for baking. In fact, she is known throughout the land for the masterpieces she creates in the kitchen. The Proper Castle has requested her skills in making their sweet-sixteen celebration cakes. So in exchange for making the cakes for the ball, I will receive an invitation.

The Same Page

As my mother and I continue to walk the cobblestone road toward the Proper Castle, I see that she is giddy with excitement. As I think of my own plans for the evening, feelings of guilt creep in. These feelings slow my pace down, and I am now a few steps behind. This is good. The less we talk, the better. I have known I will be going to a sweet-sixteen ball because of my mother's talents for baking. However, the Proper Castle's ball is not the ball I want to attend. I want to tell my mother the truth, but she will not understand. This is best. My mother will never know. Even though she has told me many times, "It's because I love you, and I just want the very best for you," her actions don't seem to back up her statements. How can she want what is best for me when she doesn't even understand me? I quickly put my feelings away and proceed with the details, playing out in my mind how I will get to the Gothic Castle tonight. It is going to be such a fun and memorable night!

As we get closer to the Proper Castle, I feel a sickness in my stomach. I hate lying to my mother but hate even more the possibility of getting caught. I catch up with her and ask, "Can we go around back, Mother?"

"Sure. Are you afraid to be seen with me?" she asks with laughter in her voice.

I can't help but roll my eyes at her.

I hear my mother talking to the servant. "Ma'am, these are the petit fours for the ball."

My thoughts wander off as she continues to talk to the servants at the castle. *How am I going to ditch my mother, not be seen by her, and get to the Gothic Castle?* My eyes quickly dart to and fro as I plan my escape. My thoughts are interrupted as my mother hands me an invitation. It's obvious how proud she is of this moment.

"Thanks, Mother. I better go."

"It seems like just yesterday you were trying on my dresses and shoes. Now look at you." In one last effort, my mother adjusts my

The Same Page

bun and halo of flowers. "Don't you want me to walk you to the front gates?" she asks.

"I can go by myself. It's not a big deal." I quickly say good-bye and begin to walk around to the front entrance. I hope she doesn't figure out why I don't want her to walk me to the front gates. Not only does she dress and look different from the other mothers, but I have no intentions of ever entering the gates of the Proper Castle.

Making sure my mother is out of sight, I move quickly and quietly toward the Gothic Castle. On my way, I hide behind a tree to change my clothes, my hair, pretty much everything about my appearance. My adrenaline rushes as I play out in my mind how the evening will go. Blade will be there, waiting for me. A nervous excitement comes over me as I picture him. He is the guy every girl wants to be noticed by. To have Blade look your way means you are something special and worthy to be noticed. I practice what I will say to him tonight and how I will flirt with him. I smile as I think of how my outfit purposely shows my figure, leaving little to the imagination. I hope all of this will make me irresistible to him.

Thinking my journey will never end, suddenly the full moon gives light to the path toward the Gothic Castle. It is finally in sight. I see honeysuckle, snatch some, and rub it along my neckline. Hoping the smell will mask my long journey from the Proper Castle, I proceed onward. I don't have an invitation to get in, but I am counting on Blade to meet me at the back gate. He is my invitation. I know he might expect something in return, but I am prepared to make some sacrifices. So with a deep breath, my shaking fist reaches up and knocks on the door.

The Same Page

I hear a deep voice from the other side of the door. "Who is it?"

"It's Ysabel." There is a pause, and I can hear my heart beating loudly as I wait to see if the door will open for me. I hear the sound of heavy metal and wood scraping as the door finally begins to open. I let out a sigh of relief and see Blade.

"I thought you would be here earlier," Blade says.

"I'm sorry," I reply as I make my way through the door.

Blade moves toward me with his expectations, and I am surprisingly uncomfortable with his forwardness. I have never seen this look in his eyes before, and I know what is on his mind. If he makes advances, how far am I willing to go? If I don't do what he wants, will it cost me the chance to be loved and admired? I have finally been noticed by a guy who is breathtaking and seems to look upon me with affection. His attention feels good.

Blade hands me a drink and leads me through the private passages toward the party.

The anticipation begins to build. Once we enter into the main Gothic courtyard where the party is being held, I am overwhelmed, trying to take everything in. I knew what to expect, but upon entering the castle, it looks and feels so different now that I'm living it. Loud music is playing by instruments I have never heard before, and other girls and guys who look like me with their dark clothes are dancing with each other in ways I have never seen before. "Why aren't you drinking that?" Blade demands, a bit of forcefulness and harshness in his voice.

"I am," I quickly reply. I put the goblet to my lips to see what all the fuss is about. As soon as it hits my lips, I want to spit it out, but I keep my composure. I feel like all eyes are on me. I have always wanted to be noticed, to be seen, but now that I am, it doesn't bring the feeling inside that I had anticipated. This is not what I want.

Blade has a smirk on his face and leaves me to join another group that is partaking in smoking something. There is laughing, smoking, dancing, and drinking, yet I notice

The Same Page

emptiness in the eyes of most. Or at least I hope I do, for I don't want to be the only one who feels this way. I have never felt more alone. I catch glances from the other girls as they look me up and down and then begin to talk about me. I feel tears begin to well up in my eyes, and once again, guilt creeps in. I must keep my composure. I have the goblet in one hand, and I slip my other hand in my pocket as my insecurities begin to take over. As I do this, I feel something in my pocket that wasn't there earlier. I pull it out; it looks like some sort of letter. I look around to see if someone is watching me, maybe someone who has given this to me. There are no eyes on me for the first time all night. I step into the moonlight to see my name beautifully written on the front. I quickly open the letter to find the words, "You are worth more than this." It is signed, "King El-Roi."

I cannot leave this Gothic party fast enough. I want to be home in my comfortable clothes, wrapped up in my mother's arms, just like when I was a child. *What am I doing?* I hear the familiar voice in my head. *Who am*

I? More importantly, where has this letter come from, and why does it have such an impact on my heart? I am going to tell Blade goodbye but realize he has already moved on to another girl at the party. How could I have been so stupid to believe he really cared about me? He obviously wanted one thing, and I shake inside as if to shake off the feelings that are beginning to creep up about my compromises. I sneak out the back gate and find myself running home. I stop at the tree where I left my white gown and make a quick change. Leaving my party clothes behind, I can't get home fast enough.

....

As I arrive on my front doorstep, I realize how great it feels to finally be home. I can't wait to go upstairs to my room and sleep off the memories of the night. As I open the front door, I begin to creep toward the staircase.

The Same Page

"Did you have fun tonight?" I hear my mother say. I am surprised to see her sitting in the worn chair in the living room.

"Yes, it was great," I answer, trying to make those words sound true.

"Well, tell me everything," my mother says with curiosity in her voice.

"There was music…gorgeous gowns… great food…" I scramble to think of what else I can say that won't necessarily be lying to my mother.

"And what about the cakes?" my mother quickly asks.

"Oh, your cakes were great. Everyone seemed to love them!" I don't know why I said that. Although I am sure it was true, which technically meant it wasn't really a lie. I try to convince myself of that.

"Did anyone comment on your dress?" my mother asks.

"Well, there definitely wasn't another one like it," I confidently say.

"I see you took your hair down."

I think she is on to me. I can feel my heart begin to beat quickly. I just need to get upstairs and end this conversation. "Mother, I'm really tired, and I think I'm going to go to bed. We can talk in the morning." This will give me some time to get my story straight.

"Why are you lying to me, Ysabel? I saw you at the Gothic Castle. I saw you have a drink. I saw you with that boy."

"What? You were there? Were you spying on me?" I can't believe her.

"That's beside the point. I am so disappointed in you! You have broken my trust. Go to your room this minute! I don't want to see you right now." My mother's tears begin to overtake her.

"Mother, I'm sorry. I wanted to tell you, but you never listen to me! And the drinking, I didn't even—"

"Not another word, young lady. Go to your room!"

I stomp up the stairs in anger and frustration. If only my mother would listen to my side of the story. I don't even think she has a heart.

"I hate you! I hate my life!" I scream through my tears as I slam my door.

The Same Page

I throw myself on the bed and bury my face in my pillow. The tears will not stop. My pillow is now stained from my black eyeliner, but I don't care. It resembles my life: a mess. I will never truly be accepted, the reflection in the mirror will never change, my mother will never trust me again, and my dreams of designing clothes will never be fulfilled.

As the salty tears begin to dry, I lay on my bed feeling hopeless. There is no use trying to sleep, so I make my way over to my mother's chest. For some reason, it's a mysterious escape every time I open the chest. Somehow, rummaging through my mother's old things has a way of bringing comfort. The chest is filled with old letters from my father to my mother when he was courting her, my mother's wedding veil, old hats, my mother's old doll, and small trinkets that must hold some kind of meaning. As I pick up the doll, memories take over, and I can't help but smile. I used to play with this same doll. As I continue to go through the chest and reach the bottom, my mother's book that has always been locked appears.

Until now, it has always seemed off limits because of the lock. But things changed tonight. Mother already invaded my privacy, so what's wrong with me invading hers? I reach for a hairpin lying on my dresser to pick the lock open. It is surprisingly easy to pick, but probably because I am so determined to discover what is inside this book. As I open it, a piece of paper falls out and floats to the floor. Intrigued by what it is, I quickly open it to find the words, "Ysabel, you are forgiven, for I make all things new." It is signed "King El-Roi."

I don't know why, but my tears are back and bigger than before. I know these words are true even though I have royally messed up. I know I can start over, and tomorrow is another day. I don't need the things castle living has to offer. Those things are not satisfying anyway. It reminds me of a letter I received in the past when I was beginning to believe lies about myself. It too was from the kingdom of El-Roi: "You are perfect just the way you are." How quickly I have forgotten that.

As I continue to wipe the tears from my eyes, I begin to look through the sketchbook.

The Same Page

At the bottom of each page is my mother's signature. It's hard to believe she has drawn these beautiful pictures of flowers.

"Why have I never seen these before?" I whisper. Her sketches are amazing. As I continue to flip through the pages, I stop at a picture of a rose that looks like it's been trampled. *Why is this picture in here among all these other flowers that seem so alive?* Written beside the rose are the words "my dreams." *Is this how my mother saw her dreams?* For the first time, I begin to see her as a real person who once had dreams of her own. My thoughts are interrupted by a knock at the door.

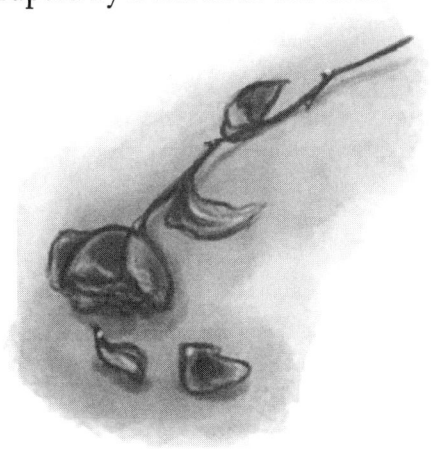

As I look up, I see my mother peeking her head in my room. I can tell that she has been crying as well.

"Can I come in?"

"Sure," I reply. There is an apparent awkwardness in the room as she makes her way to me. I have to know about these sketches.

"Mother, how come you've never shown this to me before?" I stare at my mother as she hangs her head in silence for what seems like minutes. She comes and sits next to me.

"Does it matter?" my mother replies.

"It makes all the difference," I respond.

I turn to show her the sketchbook. As she looks at it with me, I notice she is captivated by what is on the right side of the page. I hear my mother whisper to herself, "This wasn't here before." It is a note from King El-Roi: "Complete my joy by being of the same mind." My mother and I lock eyes, and without speaking a word, we seem to know what the other one is thinking. The only way we both can truly be happy and see each other through the other's eyes is to be open, honest,

· *The Same Page* ·

and to listen, not just hear. King El-Roi's thoughts towards us have a way of speaking to the heart.

"Ysabel, I know there are times when I push what I want for your life onto you. I don't take time to listen. For that, I am sorry. But, Ysabel, you really hurt me tonight. I am disappointed that you lied and deceived me. But I'm also disappointed in myself and my behavior." My mother begins to cry.

"Mother, I'm sorry too. Please don't cry. I have been so awful to you, and I'm sorry I lied and tricked you."

"Do you want to tell me what happened tonight?" my mother asks.

"Oh, Mother, it was horrible. I regret going to the Gothic Castle. I thought it offered something I wanted, but now I know better."

"Ysabel, I forgive you," my mother says as she wipes away my tears.

Still sniffling, I pick up the sketchbook. "Mother, these sketches are so good. Why have you not done anything with these?"

"That was a dream of mine that I should have chased after, but I was told it would never come to pass. My mother mocked my idea of becoming an artist. So I began to hide my drawings in this sketchbook. My dreams slowly became a secret tucked away in this book that eventually was tucked away in this chest never to be opened again. Ysabel, you have so many gifts and talents and I never want to stand in the way of your dreams."

"I don't think I have ever seen you as a real person, Mother, but as someone who has interfered and tried to ruin my life. I see things differently now. I see you differently," I honestly state.

"I love you, Ysabel," my mother says. "I will start listening to you and hearing your opinion but need you to trust me in the decisions I make as your mother. I want to give you freedom to make your own decisions. I know we both made choices that will have consequences. That happens when we are selfish. But I make a commitment, starting tonight, to celebrate who you are and help you discover all that you are intended to be."

My mother and I embrace and cry on each other's shoulders for moments that neither

The Same Page

one of us want to end. For the first time, I feel like we are both on the same page.

"We better get some rest now," my mother says.

"See you in the morning, Mother. And, Mother… I love you."

Mother kisses my forehead and picks up her sketchbook. As she is walking towards the door, she says with a wink and a smile, "May all your dreams come true." Not a night goes by that she hasn't uttered this good night wish.

"May all *our* dreams come true," I quickly reply. I mean every word.

My mother gently shuts the door behind her.

I think my heart might burst. I am so happy at this moment. As I lay my head on my pillow with the black stains my tears had made only moments before, I can't help but smile at how the night has ended. As I roll over to blow out my candle, I notice an envelope on my bedside with my name on it. It is an invitation. I quickly open it and begin to read. A tune comes to my mind, and I begin to sing it softly. I know I am living my happily ever after!

My child,

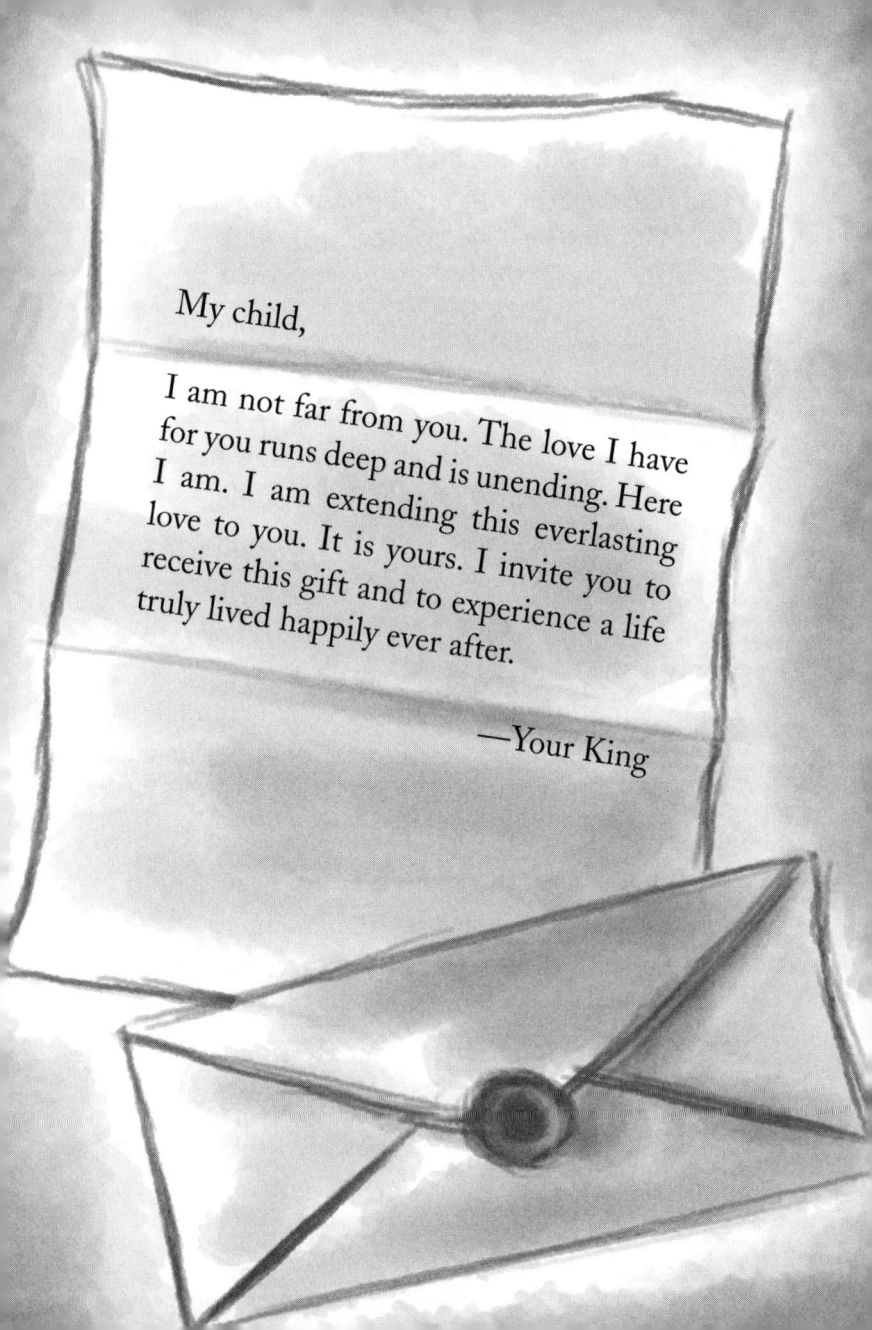

I am not far from you. The love I have for you runs deep and is unending. Here I am. I am extending this everlasting love to you. It is yours. I invite you to receive this gift and to experience a life truly lived happily ever after.

—Your King

· The Same Page ·

My response to this invitation:

_____

_____

_____

_____

_____

_____

_____

"I have loved you with an everlasting love; therefore I have continued my faithfulness to you" (Jeremiah 31:3).

Dear Masterpiece,

We have been through this journey together, *The Same Page*. Having you in mind, God has purposely taken you through these pages. So I have to ask, how are you doing? If you were to be completely honest, what would you say? It is so hard being a girl, especially a teenage girl. So many people are telling you who you are. What you're worth. And where you fit in. And in all that, you are trying to discern God's purpose for your life—and even if that's worth following. It's difficult. Especially when you have girl drama, maybe even mean-girl issues, a mom who you feel doesn't understand you—and then there are boys. Boys. That's really all I have to say. Boys can add a whole new level of insecurities and drama into your life. No wonder it's hard to listen to God's voice and His alone. There are so many other voices out there trying to get your attention. So let's be transparent for a while, shall we?

Who are you? Do you ever feel like your mom just doesn't understand? Who are you

The Same Page

trying to impress? What road are you on? What path are you choosing? Daughter of the King, oh how I wish I could give you a huge hug, look into your eyes, and tell you how precious you are, how beautiful you are, and how priceless you are! Would you believe me? You might, but if we had a friendship together, you might listen more. The same thing applies with God. He says all of these amazing truths about who you are, but if you don't have a relationship with Him, a friendship, it's hard to believe what He says.

Take some time, beloved, and honestly answer the questions on the following pages. These pages are for you, so don't waste another moment trying to pretend, fit in, and be like everyone else. You are unique, special, set apart, and individually designed. When you are finished answering the questions honestly, I want you to flip this book over and read it from Adela's perspective. It just might give you a better understanding of where your mom is coming from and how much she loves you. After you have done so, sit down with your mom and go over your answers together.

It might be awkward at first, but I promise, it will be worth it.

Perhaps it's not your mom who comes to mind when you read this book. Although in a perfect world, our relationships would be just that—perfect. But we do not live in such a place. However, we were each designed to need an older woman we can look up to and go to for support and encouragement. I pray that God will meet that need and exceed your expectations.

Praying for your relationships,
Courtney Belle Bullard

P.S. Be sure to check out Ysabel's journal at *thesamepagebook.com*.

Journal Questions and Thoughts

The times I feel most invisible…

_____

_____

_____

_____

_____

_____

"You are a God of seeing," for she said, "Truly here I have seen him who looks after me" (Genesis 16:13).

The times I feel most loved…

_____

_____

_____

_____

_____

_____

_____

"He rescued me because he delighted in me" (Psalm 18:19).

The Same Page

If I were to write a letter to my mother, I would say...

_____

_____

_____

_____

_____

_____

_____

"I thank my God in all my remembrance of you" (Philippians 1:3).

Some of my fears…

_____

_____

_____

_____

_____

_____

_____

"For God gave us a spirit not of fear but of power and love and self-control" (2 Timothy 1:7).

· *The Same Page* ·

My "happily ever after" would be...

_____

_____

_____

_____

_____

_____

_____

"May he grant you your heart's desire and fulfill all your plans" (Psalm 20:4).

If there is one thing I want my mother to know, it is…

_____

_____

_____

_____

_____

_____

_____

"Let your speech always be gracious, seasoned with salt, so that you may know how you ought to answer each person" (Colossians 4:6).

The Same Page

The times I feel empty inside…

_____

_____

_____

_____

_____

_____

_____

"My flesh and my heart may fail, but God is the strength of my heart and my portion forever" (Psalm 73:26).

When I look in the mirror, I see...

_____

_____

_____

_____

_____

_____

_____

"You are altogether beautiful, my love; there is no flaw in you" (Song of Solomon 4:7).

The Same Page

The times I feel misunderstood…

_____

_____

_____

_____

_____

_____

_____

"For the Lord sees not as man sees: man looks on the outward appearance, but the Lord looks on the heart" (1 Samuel 16:7).

Ways for my mother and me to be on the same page…

_____

_____

_____

_____

_____

_____

_____

"Complete my joy by being on the same mind, having the same love, being in full accord and of one mind" (Philippians 2:2).

What others are saying about
The Same Page

"*The Same Page* taps into the innermost thoughts and desires of every girl, no matter her age. *The Same Page* is a beautiful narrative discussion about real issues facing mothers and daughters in our world today."

—Lauren Nelson
Miss America 2007

"Though Shauna Pilgreen and Courtney Bullard wrote *The Same Page* as a fairy tale for women, it's far more! With the enchantment and wonder of great storytelling, the authors weave a charming and engaging tale that speaks directly to the reality in which women live and awakens the possibility of a greater reality they long for. Every woman wants to know she is seen by the King, and this narrative reminds a woman's heart that she is seen and known. It also provides hope that the King can bring restoration in the relationships between mothers and daughters and between women and their God.

"*The Same Page* taps into that delightful place in a woman's heart she never tires of revisiting—that place of girlish wonder. It grants far more than a good read; it facilitates an enchanting experience—especially when shared between a mother and her daughter.

"The journal pages in *The Same Page* take it past being a mere tale and prompt the reader to make it her story. Journaling allows her to inscribe her story in the pages of this story so she can experience God's story.

"I have full confidence in Shauna and Courtney as trustworthy and capable raconteurs, who not only tell a great story for mothers and daughters but tell God's great story for all women."

—Jennifer Rothschild

Author of five books, including *Lessons I Learned in the Dark, Self Talk, Soul Talk,* and three Bible studies; founder of Fresh Grounded Faith conferences.

"In our culture, mother-in-law/daughter-in-law is usually the most strained relationship. Mother/daughter runs a close second. This book from Courtney and Shauna can help temper this difficult interaction. Read this book with your daughter when she's in preschool. Read it together again when she's in grade school. Read it together again when she becomes a teenager. Read it together again when she's an adult. Encourage your daughter to read it often with her daughter. This book helps."

—Dr. John Marshall

Senior Pastor, Springfield, Missouri
Second Baptist Church

"God has decreed that spiritual truths are to 'be upon the hearts of' mothers. Then, mothers are to 'impress them' on their daughters—when they 'walk along the road, when (they) lie down and… get up.' But mothers and daughters also are to share truth when they 'sit at home.' Courtney Bullard and Shauna Pilgreen have given mothers and daughters a delightful way to do just that. *The Same Page* wraps truth in an engaging world of castles, balls, and dreams. I am certain that as both generations move through this reading and sharing experience, they will come to adore their true King in ways they never have before."

—Richard Ross, PhD

Professor of Student Ministry, Southwestern Seminary, Co-founder, True Love Waits

"Someone very wise once said that there are two great days in a person's life: the day you were born and the day you realize why. As the father of two daughters, I pray most that our girls will live from purpose and passion andnot from some confused, twisted perspective that seems to ooze from culture. Courtney and Shauna have their finger on this pulse and dive fearlessly into the deep end with this incredible resource for teenage girls and mothers. Weaving masterful story with powerful principle, this book drills to the heart of what I consider the most important issue for every girl on planet earth."

—Stuart Hall

Author of *Seven Checkpoints: 7 Principles Every Teenager Needs to Know*, *Max Q: Developing Students of Influence*, and *Wired: For a Life of Worship*

The Same Page

Kim and Ashley -
loved. that's what you are.

Shauna pilgreen

The Same Page

Living Your Happily Ever After

Shauna Pilgreen & Courtney Bullard

TATE PUBLISHING
AND ENTERPRISES, LLC

The Same Page
Copyright © 2012 by Courtney Bullard & Shauna Pilgreen. All rights reserved.

No part of this publication may be reproduced, stored in a retrieval system or transmitted in any way by any means, electronic, mechanical, photocopy, recording or otherwise without the prior permission of the author except as provided by USA copyright law.

This novel is a work of fiction. Names, descriptions, entities and incidents included in the story are products of the author's imagination. Any resemblance to actual persons, events and entities is entirely coincidental.

Scripture quotations are from The Holy Bible, English Standard Version® (ESV®), copyright © 2001 by Crossway, a publishing ministry of Good News Publishers. Used by permission. All rights reserved.

The opinions expressed by the author are not necessarily those of Tate Publishing, LLC.

Published by Tate Publishing & Enterprises, LLC
127 E. Trade Center Terrace | Mustang, Oklahoma 73064 USA
1.888.361.9473 | www.tatepublishing.com

Tate Publishing is committed to excellence in the publishing industry. The company reflects the philosophy established by the founders, based on Psalm 68:11,
"The Lord gave the word and great was the company of those who published it."

Book design copyright © 2012 by Tate Publishing, LLC. All rights reserved.
Cover and interior design by Chris Webb
Illustrations by Rebecca Riffey

Published in the United States of America

ISBN: 978-1-62024-561-3
1. Fiction / Christian / General
2. Juvenile Fiction / Historical / Medieva
12.01.17

Dedication

To the women who have poured into our lives so that we can pour into the lives of others.

To those who helped make my dreams come true...

For Ben: you spur me on to dream the unthinkable as you daily live out the dreams God has for us. It's an honor to be your wife and walk hand in hand with you.

For Elijah, Sam, and Asher: each of your moves, words, and personalities awake creativity in me to write.

For Harris and Phyllis Malcom, Natalie, and Katie: you gave me space as a quirky little girl to write Christmas programs and read you my stories.

For my family: all of you. The one I was born into. The one I married into. The ones who minister alongside us.

For Sweet Nanny and my prayer warriors: you have read urgent e-mails. You have read through our writings. But more than that, you have prayed. You have prayed boldly. You have prayed fervently.

For Courtney: whether it was being the only two girls at a writing conference that brought us together or the sheer delight we shared in stories of doing ministry with girls and moms, regardless, it's been countless moments of "jumping on the bed!"

For the girls in my life: you've sat in a small group with me. We've talked about the boy you're gonna marry. I've heard your dreams and squealed with you. We've sat in silence together trying to figure out life. You, alone and collectively, explain why God created friendship and community.

For Tate Publishing: you invited us in and helped make our book stronger.

For Jesus: You see me every second of the day and love me regardless and completely. You are the Author of my dreams and the Reason I live and breathe. Here is one of my dreams. I lay it at your feet.

—Shauna Malcom Pilgreen

Foreword from the King

My child, I love you. I adore you and truly know you better than anyone, including yourself. I know everything about you, and it doesn't change the way I see you or My love for you. Even though you sometimes run from Me, search out other things in My place, and even turn your back on Me, I am still here. I will never leave you. I will never forget you. I want to meet you right where you are. You have My full attention.

I am the King of all kings. I am the God who sees: El-Roi. I do see you. I can be trusted. I have come to offer you hope, forgiveness, and a love like no other. You are magnificent. You are My creation and I never stop thinking about you.

How do you see Me? What do you call Me? Come and sit with Me. I have so many things to reveal to you.

—King El-Roi

So she called the name of the Lord who spoke to her, "You are a God of seeing," for she said, "Truly here I have seen him who looks after me."

—Genesis 16:13

The Pages of Adela

In the blink of an eye, I find myself reminiscing of days quickly gone by. I can almost smell the wildflowers William would bring me while courting. I can feel his hands in mine. I long for the strolls he and I would take at dusk. Strolls and conversations that I never wanted to end. I would tell him of my dreams to be an artist, and he would share his dreams of being an innovator. He had a way of encouraging me to dream. He had a way of making things better. William was never satisfied with the way things had always been. Because of this peculiar way of thinking, he was shunned by the village people and certainly by my parents.

Growing up in the village, it was an acquired mindset to accept life as it had always been and not attempt to change things; unless you married up into the castle life. Even then, it wasn't a change of the mind so much as a change of status. Mother and Father had high hopes of me marrying into a castle family. They worked hard and associated with certain people in an effort for a more prestigious future for me. Yet William was a hard worker, more motivated than any other man in the land. Although it was not love at first sight, his driven and charismatic personality attracted me to him almost eighteen years ago. I longed to be loved by someone who valued who I was and my gifts within. It was my parents' rejection of my dreams that pushed me ever so closer to a younger marriage to William.

Though we lived on little, William and I were the happiest people in the land. We continued our strolls at dusk and William continued to woo me with flowers and the most creative and imaginative stories one could ever hear. A short time thereafter, I gave birth to Ysabel, and all was pleasant. This little girl added so much love to our family. Soon Ysabel was following me around, clinging to my apron strings as I would sing in the kitchen while preparing simple meals for my family.

· *The Same Page* ·

William worked the land with sweat and strength while letting his mind run wildly with innovative thoughts of making life more productive. Conversations and dreaming together had to fit in between the daily tasks of raising our daughter. Younger days were filled with baking sweets in the kitchen, dressing up like princesses, and imaginative bedtime stories. Those days seem like yesterday, yet were so long ago. How is that so?

....

My mind races back to reality as I glance up to Ysabel's window. She sits perched on that old chest of mine daydreaming again, her head in the clouds. I remember when I could just sit and dream for hours. Not today. With the potatoes I have pulled wrapped up in my apron, I walk inside, managing to open and close the door with nothing but my elbows and feet.

"Ysabel!" I call loudly. "Ysabel?"

"Ysabel, take your head out of the clouds and come downstairs!" I call again. Potatoes roll onto the countertop as I release them from the apron.

"Ysabel!" I shout it once more, startled at how quickly she appears behind me.

"I'm right here! You don't have to yell."

"Don't just stand there! There is so much work to be done," I say to her as I shake the dirt from my apron.

"Mother, I've already cleaned my room. Why do I have to clean downstairs too? This is not my house," Ysabel says to me.

My eyebrows raise. "Ysabel, as long as you live under this roof that your father and I put over your head, then you will do as I say and help with the chores. You need to be grateful for what you have." I think to myself, I've said this a time or two before.

"The castle girls are taught by tutors and don't have to get their books from the library. They own them," Ysabel argues. "They are served meals on silver platters and are not out back picking their food. Their fathers buy them whatever they want and are not away in some remote village making cents for a day's work."

The Same Page

With that comment, I hand Ysabel a brush and make a nod at the potatoes. She knows what to do. She's been scrubbing potatoes since she could barely see over the countertop.

"Do you have no appreciation for what you've been given, Ysabel?" I ask.

"Of course, I do, Mother."

I hush Ysabel with my words, "Your father is doing all he can to provide a better life for us. He wishes he could be at home, and I know you know that deep in your heart. I'm doing all I can so we can go and buy that gown for the ball."

Ysabel looks at the potatoes then back at me.

"Mother, why can't I make my own? I've got it all sketched out. You'd just have to purchase the fabric and—"

"You need to realize something early on, my dear. Your sketches will not put food on the table. You need to get your head out of the clouds and into a trade that will get you further in life." The moment these words slip from my mouth, images of *my* artwork flood my mind. I have to shake my head quickly as if to shake away the dreams of the past.

"What? Like you have a trade that's taking you further in life?" Ysabel rolls her eyes at me.

"Now, listen here. You think you're lacking, Ysabel. I've been pulling potatoes since I was six years old. I went to work for a baker at the age of nine. I want you to live the life I only dreamed of." I start to sound like my mother.

"Well, maybe that's not what I have in mind!" With that said, Ysabel puts the brush down and races out of the kitchen, leaving me tired, weary, and defeated.

"Ysabel!" I call out in frustration. It was too late. The slamming of the door stings my ears as if it had been a slap to the face.

I close my eyes and grit my teeth in disbelief to the sound that happened in unison to the door slamming. I walk with dread to the front door to discover the remains of the crash heard seconds ago.

"Not the vase!" Tears escape the corner of my eyes as I discover the remains of the vase given by my William as a wedding gift.

The Same Page

I reach down to pick up the bigger pieces. Sweeping up the rest, I see how my life resembles the shattered vase. What had once seemed like an ornate vase to hold flowers of many kinds now lay scattered on the floor in hundreds of pieces. In recent years, William has had to seek work in another village because work is scarce at home. I have quickly become head of the home, taking care of the fields, and just barely getting by. Life seems shattered.

....

Before daybreak, I wake Ysabel to begin her morning chores. I gather my things and rush to town for it is market day. Weekly, I sell our family produce and have been setting aside a portion to pay for the gown that Ysabel will wear to the ball. Though we have had to sacrifice more days of eating potatoes in every possible way, Ysabel will look radiant tonight.

The day is finally here, the day I have dreamed for my daughter. Ysabel has been invited to the sweet-sixteen ball at the Proper Castle. I so desperately want Ysabel to learn etiquette, enjoy her time tonight, and fall in love with someone who is living the castle life.

A sweet-sixteen ball is a way of celebrating your daughter's rite of passage into independence. Each castle holds a ball on the same night every year, and each ball is different.

The Gothic Castle hosts a dark and scary… tragedy is what I call it. Those attending are rebels, misfits, and lovers of the color black. Nothing good ever happens there, and what does happen will make the front page of *The Knightly News*.

The Fickle Castle's ball is swarming with young men, all who fall below my standards for my daughter. Every girl seems to have one or two by her side.

The Same Page

The Chic Castle's ball is glamorous, to say the least. I enjoy seeing the dresses and those attending this particular ball, but I have to view it from afar. Not even a year's savings could afford Ysabel the footwear for that ball.

The Proper Castle holds a fine ball. It seems to protect the innocence of a young lady while allowing her space to grow some on her own. So much has changed between me and Ysabel since her adolescent years that I don't want to face reality quite yet.

Young girls today are showing more skin, outwardly flirting with boys, and speaking their minds, even at the expense of someone's feelings and family values. Yes, that's why the Proper Castle ball is a perfect invitation.

While at market, a servant girl approaches me. "Don't forget to deliver the cakes to the east side of the castle this evening, my lady."

"Certainly. The cakes will be there on time. And the invitation?" I question her.

"Yes, if the cakes meet their approval, you will receive the invitation." The servant girl leaves as quickly as she arrived.

Ysabel's ball invitation isn't freely given. Just like other girls in the village, we have to work for ours. I have worked hard for this grand and memorable event. During my younger years, I worked for the village baker. After he passed away, an old acquaintance had seen me at market and asked if I still baked and decorated cakes. This acquaintance lives the castle life now and is on the committee to find the best cakes in the land. She sought me out months ago. I agreed to bake the best cakes, with one stipulation: an invitation to the ball for Ysabel.

· *The Same Page* ·

....

Ysabel looks breathtaking as she walks into the family room. The white gown could not fit more perfectly.

"Well, it's the night of all nights. How do I look?" Ysabel spins around in her dress.

I smile proudly, but am greatly distracted by her hair. My smile turns into a frown.

"This will not work. Go bring me your hairbrush, and let's get your hair out of your face," I say immediately.

With a few swoops of the brush and a few twists of the hair, my daughter's face is visible and radiantly outlined by a halo of flowers.

"I remember a time when I wore a dress like this and my hair was very similar. I see a little of me in you, Ysabel," I say proudly, continuing to fix her hair. Tears run down my face. "Your father would be so proud of you tonight. You know that, don't you?"

"Yes, Mother. Now, why the bun? This is so old looking."

"Young lady, a certain style is required at this ball, and we don't want to mess it up." I am firm in my answer. "Not every girl in the village will go to a ball tonight. Just think, we could be celebrating your sweet sixteen with cookies and tea just up the road at Clarice's house."

"Mother," Ysabel groans.

I move from her hair to smoothing out the wrinkles of the gown. "Tonight you could befriend a sweet girl who lives the castle life, meet a respectable young man, and impress families of prominence that might offer you an apprenticeship in town. Endless possibilities, my child." I start puffing Ysabel's sleeves.

"Mother, come on," Ysabel says to me. I can tell from her tone of voice that she is annoyed.

"You're right, Ysabel," I comment as I take a step back and admire her. I could not be happier. "You are beautiful and look like an angel. This is the big night when everything is going to be made perfect. Who knows what will become of you after the ball tonight?" I catch myself in wonderment. I can't stop dreaming my own dreams for my daughter.

The Same Page

Ysabel holds open the door and motions me outside.

I grab the boxes and exclaim, "We've got to get these cakes to the castle!"

....

I carefully tote the baker's boxes filled with delicate petit fours while Ysabel walks a few steps behind me. Because these little cakes have to be delivered early, Ysabel and I precede the castle mothers and daughters to the ball.

The village knows this is a big night for the young ladies across the kingdom. Little girls will peek out their windows soon, and young ladies will stop their chores to take notice of the parade of carriages on their way to the castles. We are still hours before such a parade. I see a few village girls and their mothers walking towards the castles. Only a few will attend from the village, and all because of a favor. Some are cooks; some are servants. Some know people who know people. I am proud to be escorting my Ysabel to the Proper Castle. Our household name will be a part of village talk tomorrow morning as having attended a castle ball. Word spreads quickly in our village. This event is a status symbol. A family matters to high society and is defined by the ball their daughter attends. What a glorious night this is!

On our walk, I take every kind gesture to heart. I make sure to catch the attention of a few as we walk. Even the men, eligible or not, take notice. I watch as they kindly tip their caps or offer a gentle wave to show their respect and approval.

Careful not to drop the boxes, I turn around to make sure Ysabel is still there. We haven't spoken since we left the house. I can only imagine that she is overwhelmed by the

The Same Page

attention as well. Ysabel has grown up so quickly. I try to hold so tightly to memories of her as a little girl, enjoying every moment of life. But I am astonished by the reality of Ysabel becoming her own person. I know I need to give her space to grow; I just don't want her to get hurt. That's why I'm always saying, "It's because I love you."

As we near the castle, Ysabel catches up with me. "Can we go around back, Mother?"

"Sure. Are you afraid to be seen with me?" I say jokingly. Ysabel answers me by rolling her eyes. Why do I tolerate this rude gesture? My mother would have thrown me in the iron cage for showing such disrespect.

The castle kitchen is full of commotion. Servants are going to and fro, making final preparations. An elderly servant sees us at the kitchen door.

"Ma'am, these are the petit fours for the ball." I open up the baker's boxes to display my work.

"Lovely," replies the servant. She takes my masterpieces and turns back toward the kitchen. "Ma'am," I try to get the servant's attention. "Ma'am." I raise my voice.

The elderly servant looks bothered to make a trip back to the kitchen entrance. "Yes?" she says.

"Yes, ma'am, my daughter was to receive an invitation to the ball once I delivered these cakes," I inform the woman.

"I see. Wait one moment." The woman comes back in a few minutes with a large, shiny envelope.

I kindly receive it from her and look at Ysabel with a magnified face. My eyebrows, smile, and forehead stretch big to show my excitement. I hand the invitation to Ysabel.

"Thanks, Mother. I better go," Ysabel says to me. I think she is genuinely grateful for the hard work that I have put into this evening. I consider it worth every bead of sweat and coin earned.

I fiddle with a few strands of Ysabel's hair that must have fallen out of place on the walk. "It seems like just yesterday you were trying on my dresses and shoes. Now look at

· *The Same Page* ·

you." I try to hold back the tears and more compliments.

"Don't you want me to walk you to the front gates?" I add.

"I can go by myself. It's not a big deal." Ysabel says good-bye as she turns away.

I nod knowing she needs to make her way to the Proper Castle entrance.

I watch as Ysabel turns the corner. I let out a sigh. I'm not quite sure if it is a sigh of relief or one of regret. Something deep down in my soul wonders if Ysabel is hiding something. On the other hand, Ysabel's heart and mind have to be filled with every emotion possible tonight: happy because of the sweet-sixteen ball, sad because her father isn't present, embarrassed because she received an invitation at the kitchen entrance, confused because she lives a village life but is about to experience castle life.

I assure myself that Ysabel is a strong young lady capable of handling these emotions. With that thought, I begin my journey home.

I travel the same way I came, taking in different sights this time. Just now am I able to notice the status, class, and society in which we are interacting. I know my daughter is in the most beautiful white gown we can afford. Ysabel is just moments away from entering the sweet-sixteen ball. However, I see that the castle girls' dresses are made from imported fabric, their hair done by professionals. They travel by carriage or horse, not by foot. What catches most of my attention is not the girls; it is their mothers. They look exquisite. It's as if they are going to the same ball as their daughters. Designer clothing, painted nails, fashionable handbags, and an intimidating image. I must have missed this memo.

Why is this bothering me so? I keep asking myself.

I pass by the fountain in the center of the square and catch a glimpse of my reflection. I don't like what I see. Up to this moment, I have been admiring the other women. Now I am comparing waistlines and figures and style.

· The Same Page ·

Out of the corner of my eye, I spot a large sale sign in the storefront of Countryside Boutique. I enter hesitantly, for I have only approached this high-end store to window shop. As I do, the little bell rings, acknowledging my presence.

"Yes, may I help you?" a voice from the rear of the store calls out.

"I'm simply looking. Thank you," I say.

"Well, isn't it a glorious night for all of the young ladies!" The saleslady continues to speak to me, making small talk. As I come into view, she is taken aback. Her demeanor changes as she realizes I'm but a mere commoner.

"Our sale items are in the back of the store. Let me know if you need anything." I feel the saleslady pass judgment on me. With a determination to prove I can shop in this store, I linger around the front where the most expensive clothing is displayed.

My eyes are drawn to a cream and coral dress. It is rich with decor and embroidery. I take the dress and confidently say, "I'd like to try this on."

The saleslady replies, "That dress?" She looks me over.

I nod again with confidence.

With the dress on, I stare at myself in the mirror. I feel so beautiful. It fits perfectly. It hides the parts I want hidden and accents the parts that I think lovely. I reach to the side to grab the tag and look at the price. My palms become instantly sweaty, and the room suddenly feels fifty degrees warmer. I look back in the mirror and refuse to talk myself out of it. I change back into my simple clothes and make my way to the counter. The saleslady is surprised that I am following through with this purchase. As she

· *The Same Page* ·

is wrapping up my splurge in delicate paper, I add to the drama. I reach for the gold belt on the accessory table.

"I'll take this as well."

I pull out every coin William has sent home from his hard-earned wages. With this purchase, there will hardly be enough money left to pay for the rest of the month's basic necessities. I take my purchase and leave the store with the little bell ringing behind me.

I find myself out on the streets again, but this time with a Countryside Boutique bag in hand. This makes all the difference. The delicate paper peeks out of the bag just right. The decorative bag catches all eyes. Simply having the bag in hand makes a statement; a statement that lets others know that I can afford to shop at Countryside Boutique, and I just did.

I feel as if I have moved up in society because of this impulse buy. A sense of pride comes over me and my judgment of others begin flooding my mind.

This judgment continues as I journey alongside the outlying areas that weave over the hills by some of the other castles. As I come near the Fickle Castle, I know that the girls who attend this ball will do anything to get the handsome young men's attention. Their dresses resemble a public park rather than a private garden—exposed and uncovered. When that much is being seen of a young lady, she becomes the object of lust rather than a treasure to be desired. I am baffled at the mothers who allow their daughters to leave home dressed this way.

Along the outskirts of the dark and dismal forest, the Gothic Castle protrudes forth, giving off a mysterious unwelcome.

"Why any child would want to be a part of that, I do not know!" I say to myself out loud.

Just as I am about to veer right, something catches my attention in the Gothic Castle courtyard. First it is the loud noise, and then it is the scene that the moonlight illuminates. I stop and stare intently at the girls laughing and partying.

"No, it can't be," I say in shock. "There's no way!"

· *The Same Page* ·

I squint my eyes for a more focused view. It is undeniably clear that Ysabel is one of the girls in the courtyard. Her hair is no longer in the bun I had styled hours earlier. She's not even in her white gown! My heart rushes with every kind of emotion. I want to run and grab Ysabel. Instead, I hide behind a bush so I can see more without being seen. I watch intently, following my daughter's every move. I see the unthinkable. Ysabel raises a goblet to her mouth and takes a drink. I don't have to wonder what's in that goblet. The Goths like it strong and hard.

The scene broadens and questions come. *Why is she with that guy? Why is she at this castle? What has happened to the daughter I thought I knew?* I could go on and on with questions that clutter my mind.

Feeling hopeless, I watch my daughter disappear into the noisy crowd. I stand no chance of being able to enter the Gothic Castle. Even if I try, I would only cause embarrassment and create more distance from my daughter. I rush home, feeling numb. I could care less at this point what others think of me and my purchase. I crave the refuge of my own home.

As I come inside, I fall down on bent knee, sobbing uncontrollably. I'm away from the crowds and feel used and deceived. I am so angry with Ysabel. I trusted her, but not anymore. I move off the floor and into the chair, my mind trying to figure out how this happened. My rapid heartbeat picks up more speed as I look at the bag still clutched in my hand. I throw the bag down in disgust.

Wait a minute, I think to myself.

The Same Page

I reach down and pick up the bag. This will get my mind off the sick feeling in my stomach concerning Ysabel. I go to my room and try on my new dress. I finish the last button and turn to face the mirror. Here I am, dressed like a castle mother and feeling totally empty inside.

What am I thinking? I wonder. I see my reflection shaking her head back and forth. I reach for the price tag, realizing I have made a ridiculous mistake.

To my surprise, on the other side of the retail price was a note that I didn't see earlier at the store.

"You're worth more than this!" It is signed "King El-Roi."

With a truth that resonates in my heart, I change into my nightgown. I carefully wrap the dress up and place it back into the bag with the belt. This impulse buy will be returned tomorrow.

I look at the Countryside Boutique bag knowing I can fix this mistake. I still have to face the issue of Ysabel. She will be returning soon and will find me waiting up.

Sounds outside startle me. I stop pacing and settle into the worn chair in the living quarters. Ysabel has come home. Will my heart stop racing long enough for me to confront her? I put my hands to my chest as if to calm my heart.

The door opens.

"Did you have fun tonight?" I ask quickly, as if to get this over with.

"Yes, it was great," Ysabel says surprisingly, but not convincingly.

"Well, tell me everything!" I say with fake enthusiasm.

"There was music...gorgeous gowns... great food..." Ysabel continues to stumble over her words.

"And what about the cakes?" I ask with ulterior motives.

"Oh, your cakes were great. Everyone seemed to love them!" Ysabel exclaims.

"Did anyone comment on your dress?" I have to know. This was Ysabel's ball and her dress, but I feel as though it was mine as well.

The Same Page

"Well, there definitely wasn't another one like it," Ysabel says.

I resent that comment. "I see you took your hair down," I say.

I can tell Ysabel is caught off guard and is struggling to come up with words immediately.

"Mother, I'm really tired, and I think I'm going to go to bed. We can talk in the morning."

I can no longer take the little white lies. "Why are you lying to me, Ysabel?" Anger accompanies my question. "I saw you at the Gothic Castle. I saw you have a drink. I saw you with that boy!"

"What? You were there? Were you spying on me?"

"That's beside the point. I am so disappointed in you! You have broken my trust. Go to your room this minute! I don't want to see you right now!" My tears overtake me.

"Mother, I'm sorry. I wanted to tell you, but you never listen to me! And the drinking, I didn't even!" Ysabel raises her voice.

I can tell she wants to defend herself as she mutters, but I give her no room to speak.

She doesn't deserve it. She has tricked me. She has possibly ruined the family name.

I raise mine too. "Not another word, young lady. Go to your room!"

She storms off upstairs. "I hate you! I hate my life!" Ysabel shouts and then slams her bedroom door.

Both of us are in utter distress and uncontrollable tears.

I sink back down into the worn chair.

I wish this night had never happened. I have many regrets. And to be honest with myself, the past regrets run deeper than those of the present. Regrets of the past reveal cutting words between me and my mother. They reveal dreams of my sketchbook never achieved because I feared rejection. And if I'm not careful, the future could hold more regrets.

During these thoughts, I find myself in a fixed stare. I blink and realize I am staring at a painting done by Ysabel when she was younger. The painting hangs simply over the fireplace across the room.

Ysabel vividly painted a picture of a land one could only dream of seeing, a land that

The Same Page

was beautiful beyond the sights of nature. Her innocent and pure painting captured the spirit of this dreamland—peaceful and restful.

I approach the painting. As I do, I spot a piece of paper sticking out from behind the canvas. I reach to pull it out.

"You were created for another Kingdom." It is signed, "King El-Roi."

I hold onto the note and sit down by the fireplace. Truths I had learned as a child and through my young adult years resurface in my heart. I know there is more to this life than designer clothing and living the castle life. I have been given a loving and healthy family. Though life has its toils and regrets, this promise I just read is true. I am not intended to fit into the castle life mold or to live beyond my means.

I know I need to make things right with Ysabel. If my daughter is going to live the best life possible, she needs to see a great example in me. I recall a note I had gotten years ago from King El-Roi that read, "Do not let the sun go down on your anger."

With that thought, I make my way to Ysabel's room. I quietly knock on her door and turn the knob to let myself in.

"Can I come in?" I ask as I peek in her room.

"Sure," Ysabel responds softly. Her face is splotchy from crying.

My daughter sits beside my old chest. This must be her place. Her place to dream. Her place to escape. Her place of refuge.

"Mother, how come you've never shown this to me before?" Ysabel asks me. As I get closer, I see she has my old sketchbook in her hands. I hang my head in silence for what seems like minutes. My sketchbook has purposefully remained locked in my old chest for years. It is in this sketchbook where I allowed my fingers to draw freely and liberally. Sketches of lavender fields, daisies, poppies, and lilies. I join Ysabel on the floor.

"Does it matter?" I wonder out loud.

"It makes all the difference," Ysabel responds.

Ysabel turns the sketchbook toward me, revealing a troubling picture. On the left is a sketch of a rose wilted and trampled upon. Words etched to the side: "my dreams." I grab

The Same Page

the corner of the book, remembering this drawing like it was yesterday. I remember my anger toward my mother. Yet just as quickly as I notice my adolescent drawing, my eyes wander to the adjoining page.

I mutter, "This wasn't here before."

It is a note from King El-Roi. "Complete my joy by being of the same mind." I glance at Ysabel. Our eyes meet. Though we say nothing, it seems as if we are thinking the same thing. We will come together when we see each other through the eyes of our King. King El-Roi's thoughts towards us have a way of speaking to the heart.

"Ysabel, I know there are times when I push what I want for your life onto you. I don't take time to listen. For that, I am sorry. But, Ysabel, you really hurt me tonight. I am disappointed that you lied and deceived me. But I am also disappointed in myself and my behavior." Tears fall naturally.

"Mother, I'm sorry too. Please don't cry. I have been so awful to you, and I'm sorry I lied and tricked you," Ysabel says to me.

"Do you want to tell me what happened tonight?"

"Oh, Mother, it was horrible. I regret going to the Gothic Castle. I thought it offered something I wanted, but now I know better," Ysabel cries.

"Ysabel, I forgive you." I wipe away my daughter's tears.

Ysabel looks back at my sketchbook. "Mother, these sketches are so good. Why have you not done anything with these?" Ysabel asks me.

"That was a dream of mine that I should have chased after, but I was told it would never come to pass," I say with hesitation. "My mother mocked my idea of becoming an artist, so I began to hide my drawings in this sketchbook. My dreams slowly became a secret tucked away in this book that eventually was tucked away in this chest, never to be opened again," I confess. "Ysabel, you have so many gifts and talents and I never want to stand in the way of your dreams."

I take the sketchbook into my hands as if a gift I am reopening.

The Same Page

"I don't think I have ever seen you as a real person, Mother, but as someone who has interfered and tried to ruin my life. I see things differently now. I see you differently," Ysabel opens up her heart to me.

"I love you, Ysabel," I begin to say. "I will start listening to you and hearing your opinion but need you to trust me in the decisions I make as your mother. I want to give you freedom to make your own decisions. I know we both made choices that will have consequences. That happens when we are selfish. But I make a commitment, starting tonight, to celebrate who you are and help you discover all that you are intended to be."

Ysabel and I share a much-needed, long embrace. This embrace doesn't mean that tomorrow will be easier or that the hardest decisions are over. It does, however, put us on the same page.

"We better get some rest now," I say.

"See you in the morning, Mother. And, Mother... I love you." Ysabel says genuinely.

I give Ysabel a kiss on the forehead and pick up my sketchbook.

"May all your dreams come true," I say with a wink and a smile. I've uttered this good night wish every night for the past sixteen years to my sweet girl. This night I meant every word.

"May all *our* dreams come true," Ysabel replies quickly. I couldn't agree more.

I gently close the door behind me. I glance down at my sketchbook. It will not be returned to the chest, for I am ready to be reacquainted with my dreams. That will have to wait until tomorrow, for I am tired. The years are short, but the days seem long sometimes. Today was one of those days.

Before I blow out the candle, I find an invitation leaning against the base of the candle stand. The invitation has my name on it. I open it and smile and nod. I blow out the candle and rest my head on the pillow. My sketchbook and invitation I hold close to my heart. Tears begin to run down the side of my face into my ear and onto the pillow, tears of joy, for I realize I am living my happily ever after.

My child,

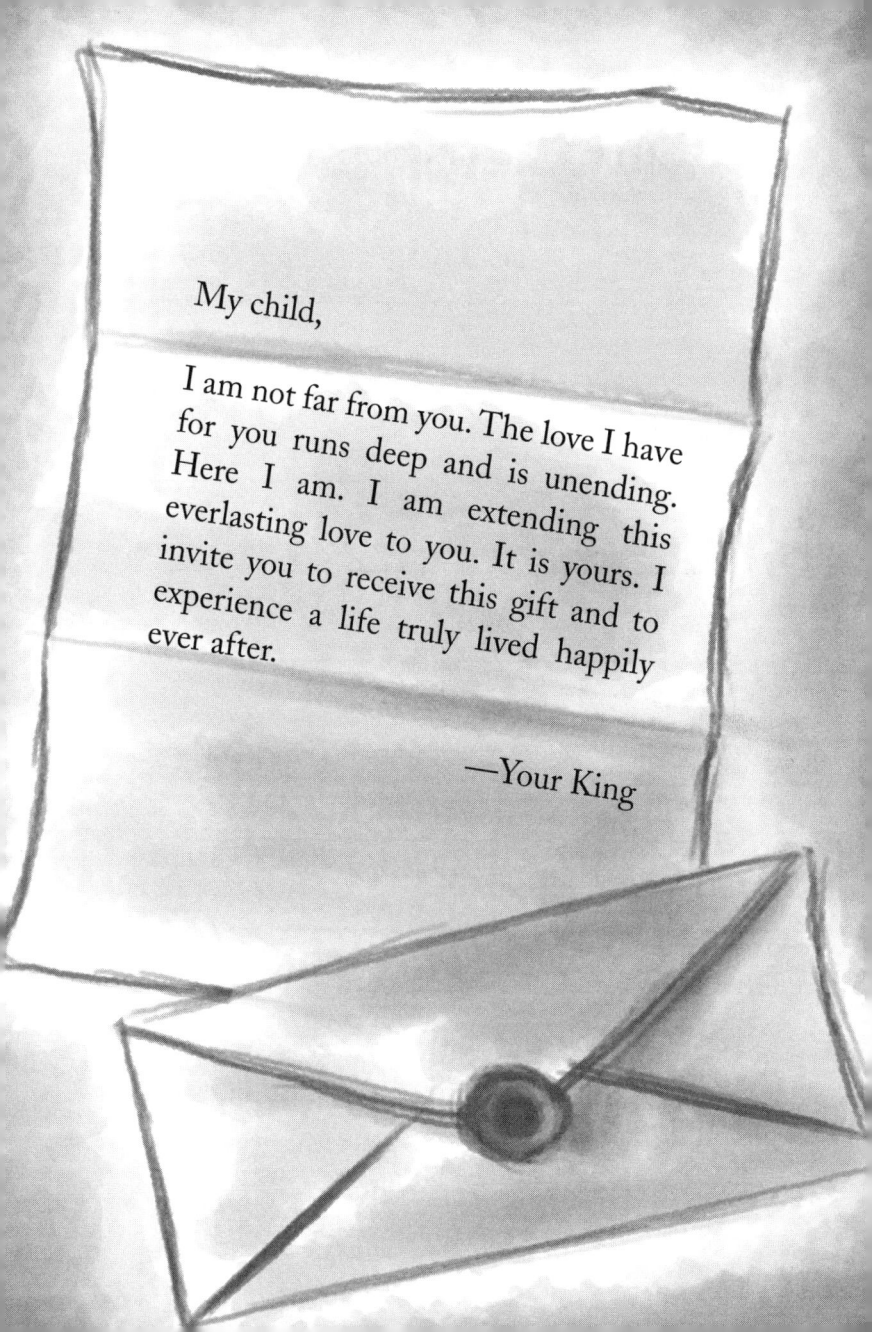

I am not far from you. The love I have for you runs deep and is unending. Here I am. I am extending this everlasting love to you. It is yours. I invite you to receive this gift and to experience a life truly lived happily ever after.

—Your King

My response to this invitation:

_____

_____

_____

_____

_____

_____

_____

"I have loved you with an everlasting love; therefore I have continued my faithfulness to you" (Jeremiah 31:3).

The Same Page

Dear Seen One,

God sees you and me. He loves us. Let that truth bring you comfort in this very moment. Even if God seems far, this is still true. Even if you are searching, He knows you intricately. God knows your daughter as well. He crafted the relationship between the two of you. He purposefully chose you to lead her in the way she should go. He, as your Father, is cheering for you.

My friend, I have been praying for you. I am on this journey with you, and what a journey we find ourselves on today! The load we carry with us is full of all types of emotions, from being scared, frustrated, or content one minute, distracted or weary the next, to trusting here and wishy-washy there. When you and I carry all of these emotions inside, we crowd up the space where God intends to display grace, hope, joy, and peace. Emotions rise and fall based on what we experience and are feeling. But we don't have to let those emotions determine our actions. Instead, let's exchange our flighty emotions for truth. For when we stand on truth, we can follow our dreams.

Often, it's everyone else's loads we're carrying, and we've laid ours down along the way. Take a look behind you. Keep looking back. What was life like at eight years old? Remember how the world looked? Think about your teenage years. First crush. Attempting to put mascara on. Driving by yourself. And that style. What were we wearing? It's in our childhood when we were discovering life as girls, that gifts and talents were being unveiled. You threw the ball up and scored. You twirled, and it felt beautiful. You got a grade back on a test and were pleased. Those days of discoveries look quite different now. But let me remind you, those childhood days, those talents, those dreams—they are gifts to you from God, the Giver of all good things. And He's not finished with you yet.

Where was that moment in Adela's story where you paused, making a connection in your own life? Much of Adela's journey resonates within me. As a woman, wife, and mom, I fight the status quo. I wrestle internally

The Same Page

with desires to want more, obtain more, and succeed more. I squirm during moments I'm given to be still. I see my passions and gifts sitting to the side while I raise children to pursue their passions and gifts. God doesn't intend for your life to be on hold. You and I both have dreams of our own that are still within us.

The questions that follow this letter are for you to answer honestly. Take a deep breath and see yourself the way your King sees you. As His child, you have the incredible freedom to let go and get real in His presence. Search for Him and find Him. Dig through that chest of yours and lay bare your dreams and desires for yourself and for your family. Afterwards, read Ysabel's story and appreciate her viewpoint. Ask for favor as you approach your daughter, then ask God to heal, mend, and restore.

Perhaps your daughter is wayward. You are still her mother. I know it's hard, but I beg you to persevere. Change doesn't happen overnight. Just as your King seeks restoration with you, pursue your daughter. God sees her and loves her in this moment. Pray for courage and strength to do the same.

Know that to have a relationship, you have to have conversation. To have conversation, you have to listen. To listen, you have to be selfless. Her responding to you greatly depends on your relationship. I challenge you to listen to your daughter as she shares her thoughts. Take the time to be honest with her about your fears and dreams. Embrace and live out the faith journey together.

> On the journey with you,
> Shauna Pilgreen

P.S. Be sure to check out Adela's journal at *thesamepagebook.com*.

Journal Questions and Thoughts

The times I feel misunderstood…

_____

_____

_____

_____

_____

_____

_____

"For the Lord sees not as man sees: man looks on the outward appearance, but the Lord looks on the heart" (1 Samuel 16:7).

When I look in the mirror, I see...

_____

_____

_____

_____

_____

_____

_____

"You are altogether beautiful, my love; there is no flaw in you" (Song of Solomon 4:7).

· *The Same Page* ·

The times I feel empty inside...

_____

_____

_____

_____

_____

_____

_____

"My flesh and my heart may fail, but God is the strength of my heart and my portion forever" (Psalm 73:26).

If there is one thing I want my daughter to know, it is…

_____

_____

_____

_____

_____

_____

_____

"Let your speech always be gracious, seasoned with salt, so that you may know how you ought to answer each person" (Colossians 4:6).

· The Same Page ·

My "happily ever after" would be...

_____

_____

_____

_____

_____

_____

_____

"May he grant you your heart's desire and fulfill all your plans" (Psalm 20:4).

Some of my fears...

_____

_____

_____

_____

_____

_____

_____

_____

"For God gave us a spirit not of fear but of power and love and self-control" (2 Timothy 1:7).

· The Same Page ·

If I were to write a letter to my daughter, I would say…

_____

_____

_____

_____

_____

_____

_____

"I thank my God in all my remembrance of you" (Philippians 1:3).

The times I feel most loved…

_____

_____

_____

_____

_____

_____

_____

"He rescued me because he delighted in me" (Psalm 18:19).

· The Same Page ·

The times I feel most invisible...

_____

_____

_____

_____

_____

_____

_____

"You are a God of seeing," for she said, "Truly here I have seen him who looks after me" (Genesis 16:13).

Ways for me and my daughter to be on the same page...

_____

_____

_____

_____

_____

_____

_____

"Complete my joy by being on the same mind, having the same love, being in full accord and of one mind" (Philippians 2:2).